James Clarence Harvey

Lines and Rhymes

Grave and gay

James Clarence Harvey

Lines and Rhymes
Grave and gay

ISBN/EAN: 9783337272548

Printed in Europe, USA, Canada, Australia, Japan

Cover: Foto ©Andreas Hilbeck / pixelio.de

More available books at **www.hansebooks.com**

LINES AND RHYMES.

GRAVE AND GAY,

BY

JAMES CLARENCE HARVEY.

SELECTED AND PUBLISHED BECAUSE OF THEIR
ADAPTABILITY FOR PUBLIC RECITA-
TION AND READING.

NEW YORK

FRANK F. LOVELL & COMPANY

142 AND 144 WORTH STREET

Dedication.

TO MY MOTHER.

J. C. H.

TABLE OF CONTENTS.

LINES AND RHYMES.

A ROMAN LEGEND.

Hour by hour, with skilful pencil, wrought the
    artist, sad and lone,
Day by day, he labored nobly, though to all the
    world unknown,
He was brave, the youthful artist, but his soul
    grew weak and faint,
As he strove to place before him, the fair features
    of a saint,
Worn and weary, he strove vainly, for the touch
    of Heavenly grace,
Till, one day, a radiant sunbeam fell upon the up-
    turned face,
And the very air was flooded with a presence
    strangely sweet,
For the soul, within the sunbeam, seemed to make
    the work complete,
Swift as thought, the artist's pencil deftly touched
    the features fair,
Night came down, but one bright sunbeam left its
    soul imprisoned there ;

And around his dingy garret, gazed the artist,
    wondering,
For the work sublime illumed it, like the palace
    of a king;
And within the artist nature, flamed his first, fond
    love divine,
Which bewildered all his senses, as with rare, old,
    ruby wine.
Yearningly, he cried : " I love thee," to the radiant,
    saintly face,
But the never-ceasing answer was a look of Heav-
    enly grace.
Out into the world he wandered, questioning,
    searching everywhere,
And the stars above, full often, heard his soul burst
    forth in prayer:
" God in Heaven, in mercy, hear me! Hear thy
    suppliant's pleading cry,
Lead, oh! lead my footsteps to her. Grant but
    this, or let me die."
Friends forsook and want pursued him, still he
    struggled on, alone,
Till, at last, outworn and trembling, reason tot-
    tered on its throne,
And he seemed the helpless plaything of some
    mad, relentless fate,
Till the Sisterhood of Mercy found him lying at
    their gate;
Made him welcome, gave him shelter and with
    ever-patient care
Bathed his brow and brushed the tangled, matted
    tresses of his hair.

Long he lingered on the borders of the holy-land
    of death,
One fair Sister, by his bedside, counting low each
    fluttering breath.
Softly fell the evening shadows, shutting out the
    golden glow,
Of a gorgeous, lingering sunset, gilding all the
    earth below,
When, upon his pillow turning, swift came to him
    hope's bright gleams,
For the anxious face, above him, was the loved
    one of his dreams.
But her life was one of mercy and the band across
    her brow,
Gave the spotless testimony of a maiden's holy
    vow.
" Is this Heaven? Are you an angel ? " swift
    he questioned her, the while,
She smoothed back his wavy tresses, only answer-
    ing with a smile;
" Tell me truly, couldst thou love me, since thou
    wouldst not let me die ? "
But she pointed to the band about her brow and
    breathed a sigh.
In her hours of patient watching, she had learned
    the bitter truth,
That the Sisterhood of Mercy has its anguish and
    its ruth ;
Nevermore she came, well-knowing, from tempta-
    tion she must fly,
For his eager, tender questions, in her heart, had
    found reply.

Every morning, he would question: " Will she come
   to me to-day ? "
And the tender, truthful Sisters shook their heads
   and turned away,
For adown his classic features passed the shadow
   of his pain,
As he closed his eyes and murmured: " She will
   never come again."
In his dreams, one night, he fancied she had bent
   above his bed,
And his longing arms reached upward, but the
   vision sweet had fled.
Hopeless, in his great heart-hunger, through a
   storm of wind and rain,
To his picture turned the artist, bowing low, with
   grief and pain ;
Open wide, he threw the shutters of his garret
   casement high,
Heeding not the vivid lightning, as it flashed
   athwart the sky.
On his lowly couch reclining, soon in weariness,
   he slept,
While the storm clouds o'er him thundering, long
   and loud their vigils kept.
Wilder grew the night and fiercer blew the winds,
   until, at last,
Like a bird of prey or demon, through the shat-
   tered casement, passed
The old shutter, rending, tearing every wondrous
   touch and trace
Of the artist's patient labor, from the radiant,
   saintly face ;

And the jagged bands of lightning, as they flashed
  along the floor,
Lit the crushed and crumpled canvas, worthless
  now, forevermore.
And the artist, slowly rising, groped his way across
  the room,
Feeling, knowing he had lost her, though en-
  shrouded in the gloom.
Then he sought his couch and murmured: "It is
  well, God knoweth best."
And the sunbeams of the morning found a weary
  soul—at rest.

THE WHISTLING REGIMENT.

[In the recitation which follows, the effect can be heightened by an accompaniment on the piano and by the whistling of strains from Annie Laurie, adapting the style to the sentiment of the verses. The melody should be played very softly, except where the battle is alluded to, and the whistling should be so timed that the last strain of Annie Laurie may end with the words, "would lay me down and die." The beat of the drums can be introduced with good effect, but it is better to omit it unless it can be done skilfully. It is well to state before reciting, that the escape described is not entirely imaginary, as many prisoners made their way through underground passages from rebel prisons, during the Civil War. An asterisk at the end of a line denotes where the whistling should commence, and a dagger where it should cease.]

When the North and South had parted, and the
    boom of the signal gun
Had wakened the Northern heroes, for the great
    deeds to be done,
When the nation's cry for soldiers had echoed o'er
    hill and dale,
When hot youth flushed with courage, while the
    mother's cheeks turned pale,
In the woods of old New England, as the day sank
    down the west,
A loved one stood beside me, her brown head on
    my breast.
From the earliest hours of childhood our paths
    had been as one,
Her heart was in my keeping, though I knew not
    when 'twas won:

We had learned to love each other, in a half un-
    spoken way,
But it ripened to full completeness when the
    parting came, that day;
Not a tear in the eyes of azure, but a deep and
    fervent prayer,
That seemed to say: " God bless you, and guard
    you, everywhere."
At the call for volunteers, her face was like drifted
    snow.
She read in my eyes a question and her loyal heart
    said, " Go,"
As the roll of the drums drew nearer, through the
    leaves of the rustling trees,*
The strains of Annie Laurie were borne to us, on
    the breeze.
Then I drew her pale face nearer and said : " Brave
    heart and true,
Your tender love and prayers shall bring me back
    to you."
And I called her *my* Annie Laurie and whispered
    to her that I
For her sweet sake was willing—to lay me down
    and die
And I said: " Through the days of danger, that
    little song shall be
Like a pass word from this hillside, to bring your
    love to me." †
Oh! many a time, at nightfall, in the very shades
    of death,
When the picket lines were pacing their rounds
    with bated breath,*

The lips of strong men trembled and brave breasts
    heaved a sigh,
When some one whistled softly; " I'd lay me down
    and die." †
The tender little ballad our watch-word soon be-
    came
And in place of Annie Laurie, each had a loved
    one's name.
In the very front of battle, where the bullets thick-
    est fly,*
The boys from old New England oft-times went
    rushing by,
And the rebel lines before us gave way where'er
    we went,
For the gray coats fled, in terror, from the " whis-
    tling regiment."
Amidst the roar of the cannon, and the shriek of
    the shells on high,
You could hear the brave boys whistling: " I'd
    lay me down and die." †
But, Alas! Though truth is mighty and right will,
    at last, prevail,
There are times when the best and bravest, by the
    wrong outnumbered, fail;
And thus, one day, in a skirmish, but a half-hour's
    fight at most,
A score of the whistling soldiers were caught by
    the rebel host.
With hands tied fast behind us, we were dragged
    to a prison pen,
Where, hollow-eyed and starving, lay a thousand
    loyal men.

No roof but the vault of Heaven, no bed save the
    beaten sod,
Shut in from the world around us, by a wall where
    the sentries trod,
For a time, our Annie Laurie brought cheer to
    that prison pen;
A hope to the hearts of the living; a smile to the
    dying men.
But the spark of Hope burned dimly, when each
    day's setting sun
Dropped the pall of night o'er a comrade, whose
    sands of life were run.
One night, in a dismal corner, where the shadows
    darkest fell,
We huddled close together, to hear a soldier
    tell
The tales of dear New England and of loved ones
    waiting there,
When, Hark! a soft, low whistle, pierced through
    the heavy air,*
And the strain was Annie Laurie. Each caught
    the other's eye,
And with trembling lips we answered: "I'd lay
    me down and die."
From the earth, near the wall behind us, a hand
    came struggling through,
With a crumpled bit of paper for the captive boys
    in blue.
And the name! My God! 'Twas Annie, my Annie,
    true and brave,
From the hills of old New England she had fol-
    lowed me to save.†

"Not a word or a sign, but follow, where'er you
  may be led,
Bring four of your comrades with you," was all
  that the writing said.
Only eight were left of the twenty and lots were
  quickly thrown,
Then our trembling fingers widened the space
  where the hand had shown.
With a stealthy glance at the sentries, the prisoners
  gathered round,
And the five whom fate had chosen stole silent
  underground,
On, on, through the damp earth creeping, we followed our dusky guide,
Till under a bank o'erhanging, we came to the
  riverside:
"Straight over," a low voice whispered, "where
  you see yon beacon light."
And ere we could say: "God bless you," he van-
  ished into the night.
Through the fog and damp of the river, when the
  moon was hid from sight,
With a fond, old, faithful negro, brave Annie had
  crossed each night;
And the long, dark, narrow passage had grown till
  we heard close by
The notes of the dear old pass-word: "I'd lay me
  down and die."
With oar-locks muffled and silent, we pushed out
  into the stream,
When a shot rang out on the stillness. We could
  see by the musket gleam,

A single sentry firing, but the balls passed harm-
    less by,
For the stars had hid their faces and clouds swept
    o'er the sky.
O God! How that beacon burning, brought joy
    to my heart, that night,*
For I knew whose hand had kindled that fire to
    guide our flight.
The new-born hope of freedom filled every arm
    with strength,
And we pulled at the oars like giants till the shore
    was reached at length.
We sprang from the skiff, half fainting, once
    more in the land of the free,
And the lips of my love were waiting to welcome
    and comfort me.
In my wasted arms I held her, while the weary
    boys close by
Breathed low, "For Annie Laurie, I'd lay me
    down and die." †

AT THE STAGE DOOR.

THE curtain had fallen, the lights were dim,
    The rain came down with a steady pour;
A white-haired man, with a kindly face,
    Peered through the panes of the old stage door.
" I'm getting too old to be drenched like that,"
    He muttered and turning, met face to face,
The woman whose genius, an hour before,
    Like a mighty power, had filled the place.

" Yes, much too old," with a smile, she said,
    And she laid her hand on his silver hair;
" You shall ride with me to your home to-night,
    For that is my carriage standing there."
The old door-tender stood, doffing his hat
    And holding the door, but she would not stir,
Though he said it was not for the " likes of him
    To ride in a kerridge with such as her."

" Come, put out your lights," she said to him,
    " I've something important I wish to say,
And I can't stand here in the draught you know—
    I can tell you much better while on the way."
So into the carriage the old man crept,
    Thanking her gratefully, o'er and o'er,
Till she bade him listen while she would tell
    A story, concerning that old stage door.

" It was raining in torrents, ten years ago
    This very night, and a friendless child
Stood, shivering there, by that old stage door,
    Dreading her walk, in a night so wild.
She was only one of the ' extra ' girls,
    But you gave her a nickel to take the car,
And said ' Heaven bless, ye, my little one,
    Ye can pay me back ef ye ever star.'

" So you cast your bread on the waters then,
    And I pay you back, as my heart demands,
And we're even now—no! not quite," she said,
    As she emptied her purse in his trembling hands.
"And if ever you're needy and want a friend,
    You know where to come, for your little mite
Put hope in my heart and made me strive
    To gain the success you have seen to-night."

Then the carriage stopped, at the old man's door,
    And the gas-light shone on him, standing there;
And he stepped to the curb, as she rolled away,
    While his thin lips murmured a fervent prayer,
He looked at the silver and bills and gold,
    And he said: "She gives all this to me?
My bread has come back a thousandfold,
    God bless her! God bless all such as she!"

WHY.

WHY do I love thee? Ask the flower,
  That nods by the woodland stream,
Why it loves the light of the morning sun
  And kisses each golden beam;
Ask of the blushing clover bloom,
  In the light of the dawning day,
Why it presses the dew-drop close to its breast
  And droops when it steals away.

Ask why the moonbeams kiss the sea,
  Why the lily loves the rain,
Why the morning glory bares its breast,
  When the sunshine comes again.
Ask why the song bird loves its mate,
  Why the daisies love the lea;
And learn from them, they'll tell thee true,
  Why thou art dear to me.

A LEGEND OF THE IVY.

In a quiet village of Germany, once dwelt a fair-
   haired maiden,
Whose eyes were as blue as the summer sky and
   whose hair with gold was laden ;
Her lips were as red as a rose-bud sweet, with
   teeth, like pearls, behind them,
Her smiles were like dreams of bliss, complete,
   and her waving curls enshrined them.
Fond lovers thronged to the maiden's side, but of
   all the youth around her,
One only had asked her to be his bride, and a
   willing listener found her.
"Some time, we'll marry," she often said, then
   burst into song or laughter,
And tripped away, while the lover's head hung low
   as he followed after.
Impatient growing, at last he said : "The spring-
   time birds are mating,
Pray whisper, sweet, our day to wed; warm hearts
   grow cold from waiting,"
"Not yet," she smiled, with a fond caress; but he
   answered. "Now or never.
I start for the Holy War unless I may call thee
   mine forever."

" For the Holy War ?   Farewell! " she cried, with
    never a thought of grieving.
His wish so often had been denied, she could not
    help believing
His heart would wait, till her budding life had
    blown to its full completeness.
She did not know that a wedded wife holds a
    spell in her youthful sweetness.
But alas! for the " Yes " too long delayed, he
    fought and he bravely perished;
And alas! for the heart of the tender maid, and
    the love it fondly cherished;
Her smile grew sad for all hope was gone; life's
    sands were swiftly fleeting.
And just at the break of a wintry dawn, her broken
    heart ceased beating;
And when, on her grave, at the early spring,
    bright flowers her friends were throwing,
They knelt and there, just blossoming, they saw a
    strange plant growing,
Its tender fingers, at first, just seen, crept on
    through the grass and clover,
Till, at last, with a mound of perfect green, it
    covered the whole grave over,
And often the village youth would stand by the
    vine-clad mound, in the gloaming,
And holding a maiden's willing hand, would tell
    that the strange plant roaming,
Was the maiden's soul, which could not rest and
    with fruitless, fond endeavor,
Went seeking the heart it loved the best, but
    sought in vain, forever.

SOCIETY'S CENTENNIAL.

MADAME VAN GUYSTER was rosy and plump,
  Rosy and pretty was she.
Mr. Van Guyster was portly and red,
  Portly and gruff was he.
" Beautiful match," all the people had said
When pretty and portly, the two were wed,
Yet a cat and dog life was the life they led,
                    Ah me!

Madame loved dearly society calls,
  Charity fairs and all that;
Danced with delight at Inaugural Balls,
  Raved o'er a new Easter hat.
And didn't mind flirting a bit now and then,
At just the right time with the right kind of men.
But Van Guyster said: "Wait till she does it
    again,
                    We'll see!"

April came 'round with its showers and its sun;
  Madame went driving one day,
Her only companion a French marquis,
  Known to be rapid and gay.
So Mr. Van Guyster concluded to dine
Down at the club and get flushed with wine:
That he was upset, 'twas a very sure sign,
                    Though rare.

"Mrs. Van Guyster!" he said, with a frown,
  "Flirt if you must and you will.
Here is a letter which says that you dance,
  Dance in the famous quadrille,
Here are the tickets and here is the way,
Your little coquetries I shall repay,
You shall stay home on that auspicious day,
                    I swear!"

Slightly unsteady, he strode to the grate;
  Flourished the cards in the air;
Calling attention to what he was at,
  Then he proceeded to tear.
He tore up the tickets in wee little bits,
He turned and he gave her particular fits,
Mrs. Van Guyster scared out of her wits,
                    Stood dumb.

Never before had connubial bliss
  Taken this tragical turn;
What had occasioned an outburst like this,
  She was unable to learn.
Quickly she rallied and sweetly she said:
"Mr. Van Guyster, you're out of your head.
I shall go to the ball, sir, unless I am dead,
                    Now come!"

Scarcely believing he meant what he said,
  Think of the lady's surprise,
Early next morning, to see all her trunks
  Carted off, under her eyes;

Costumes sent flying, right under her nose,
Even her boots and her dainty silk hose,
She was nigh crazy, as you may suppose,
             Poor thing!

Mr. Van Guyster, at last, went away,
   Turning the key in the door.
Mrs. Van Guyster then had a good cry,
   Curled in a heap on the floor,
"This is my punishment," softly she cried,
"These are the tears that all women betide,
Who insist on becoming some wealthy man's bride,
            Oh! The sting!"

All of a sudden she sprang to her feet,
   Fire flashing bright in her eye,
Pearly white teeth were set tight as she said:
   "I'll go to that ball if I die!"
Up through the air shaft she summoned her maid,
Pulled down the hangings of satin brocade,
Over them, dainty lace curtains were laid,
            So neat!

Scissors and needles and silks were at hand,
   Oh! How they worked on that dress,
Slashing and cutting up hangings that cost
   Half a small fortune, I guess,
Over her shoulders the garment was flung,
To her anatomy softly it clung,
Gracefully! Well! I can't tell with my tongue,
            How sweet!

Then on a ladder, out into the yard
  Mrs. Van Guyster went down,
Dainty, pink ankles exposing, of course,
  They were the talk of the town.
Into a carriage she sprang with a dash,
" Drive to the shoe store of Mr. De Cash! "
Mr. Van Guyster threw open the sash,
                    And swore.

Swore by George Washington, Martha as well,
  Swore by the point of his knife,
Swore by the sacred four hundred that he
  Would frustrate the plan of his wife.
Hastily dressing, he flew to the ball,
Stood like a statue, up close to the wall,
Stately and grim and bald-headed and tall,
                    By the door.

Distant, sweet music at last, from within,
  Smote on his listening ear,
The famous cotillion was on then and she,--
  She was outwitted, 'twas clear.
He chuckled and opened a bottle in glee,
Went in to the ball, when Lo! who should he see!
His wife on the arm of the French marquis,
                    Great Scott!

Mr. Van Guyster, with jealousy wild,
  Sprang at his throat with a scream;
All was confusion and then—he awoke,
  Out of a troublesome dream.
Mr. Van Guyster had dined as I said,
Mrs. Van Guyster was rubbing his head,
Since then a much pleasanter life they have led,
                    Why not!

TWO ROSES.

BENEATH thy open window, sweet,
   I stood, last night. The stars, on high,
   Peeped through the rift clouds, sailing by,
To light my wandering, love-led feet
     Along the path where roses white
     Gave to the breezes of the night
     A kiss of fragrance, soft and light,
With which thy sleeping smile to greet.
     And as thy curtains softly swayed,
     With fervent lips, sweet love, I prayed,
     The warm night wind would breathe to thee
     How Heavenly dear thou art to me.

I plucked two roses, blooming there,
   One, purest white, one, deepest red,
   Thy love and mine, interpreted,
And flung them, through the odorous air,
     Naught thinking, caring naught but this,
     One bore to thee a lover's kiss
     To tinge, perchance, a dream of bliss
And nestle in thy golden hair;
     The rich, red rose, thy heart would keep;
     It told of passion strong and deep,
     And well I knew thy lips would find
     The kiss within, though love be blind.

And while I lingered, lovingly,
        Content with thoughts that thou wert near
        E'en though thy voice I could not hear,
A sweet surprise flew forth from thee.
            The pure, white rose that I had thrown,
            Against my breast was gently blown,
            And bore a kiss from thee, my own.
To gladden and enrapture me.
            Swift lips, against the petals fair,
            Pressed close the kiss, imprisoned there,
            And down the path, the roses white,
            Heard whispered low: " My love, Good-night."

THE WAXEN BUST.

Mr. LENSLY DE JONES was a timid man,
  Who stammered whenever he talked,
It affected his gait, for he hippity-hopped
  Where other people walked.

Now Lensly de Jones was a wonderful man,
  In the photographic art,
He wasn't the chief in the Grand Salon,
  But he played a prominent part.

And the day that the Grand Mogul was ill
  With a touch of the gout, they say,
Victoria Regina was out for a drive
  And happened to pass that way.

" What ho! " quoth the Queen, " I'm in face to-day
  I' faith! I am looking well,
Many years I shall reign and a photograph,
  To my subjects, this fact shall tell."

So into the hall of the Grand Salon,
  Swept the Queen with her retinue,
And Lensly de Jones was so terrified
  That he didn't know what to do.

He stammered: "G-G-Good-day" and stuttered:
    " p-pray s-sit,"
And stumbled all over the room,
And he jumped when Her Majesty spoke to him
    As though 'twas the crack-o-doom.

There wasn't a man in the British Isles
    As skilful as he, I ween,
In preparing a first-class photograph
    For any one but his Queen.

But he couldn't say " Lift up your chin " to her,
    He couldn't command her smiles,
He couldn't put prongs in the back of the hea
    Of the Queen of the British Isles.

She was out of focus, the light was bad,
    And her head was moving too;
And Lensly de Jones felt a *positive* dread
    Lest the *negative* might not do.

But he trundled the camera to and fro,
    And then he exposed the plate,
And promised the proofs as the Queen rode off,
    Leaving Lensly stammering: " W-wait."

Instead of the sensitive plates they used,
    What think you the man had done!
Put in a tin sign which the legend bore:
    "At dinner. Be back at one."

All day and all night, with a pan of wax,
    Poor Lensly might have been seen,
With deep solicitude, modelling
    A bust of the gracious Queen.

And when it was done it was photographed
 And the proofs much pleased the Queen,
For Lensly had flattered her dreadfully,
 With a face sedate, serene.

The House of Lords with a single voice
 Made Lensly a belted knight.
They sent him the news one afternoon
 And the poor man died of fright.

Thus endeth the tale of the photograph
 Of England's gracious Queen,
And the waxen bust of the belted knight,
 With the face sedate, serene.

THE BICYCLE RIDE.

[Whether bicycle riding on Sunday be sinful or not, depends entirely upon the spirit in which it is done and the associations of the ride.—EDITOR'S OUTING.]

You have read of the ride of Paul Revere,
And of Gilpin's ride, so fraught with fear;
Skipper Ireson's ride in a cart,
And the ride where Sheridan played a part;
Calendar's ride on a brazen hack,
And Islam's prophet on Al Borak;
The fateful ride to Aix from Ghent,
And a dozen others of like portent,
But you never have heard of a bicycle spin
Which was piously ended, though started in sin.

Tom was a country parson's son,
Fresh from college and full of fun,
Fond of flirting with bright-eyed girls,
Raving, in verse, over golden curls,
Sowing a wild oat, here and there,
In a way that made the parson stare
And chide him sternly, when face to face,
While, in private, he laughed at the young scape-
    grace.
But the wildest passion the boy could feel
Was the love he bore for his shining wheel.

He rode it by night and he rode it by day,
If he went two rods or ten miles away;
And Deacon Smith was heard to remark
That he met that "pesky thing in the dark
And it went right by with a glint and a gleam
And a wild 'hoot-toot' that made him scream;
In spite of the fact that he knew right well
That evil spirits were all in—well—
He wouldn't meet that thing again
For a corn-crib full of good, ripe grain."

One Sunday morning, the sun was bright,
The birds' throats bursting with glad delight,
The parson mounted his plump old bay
And jogged to the church, two miles away,
While Tom wheeled round, ten miles or more
And hid his wheel by the chancel door,
And he thought, as he sat in the parson's pew,
" I wonder what makes dad look so blue."
Till it came like a flash to his active mind,
He'd left his sermon and specs behind.

Now the parson was old and his eyes were dim
And he couldn't have read a line or a hymn.
Without his specs, for a mint of gold,
And his head turned hot while his toes turned cold,
And right in the midst of his mental shock,
The parson deceived his trusting flock,
And gave them eternal life and a crown
From the book he was holding upside down,
Tom, the rascal, five minutes before,
Like an arrow had shot from the chancel door.

The horses he frightened I never can tell,
Nor how the old church folks were shocked, as well,
And they said they feared that the parson's lad
" Was a-gettin' wild " and would go to the bad,
For 'twas wicked enough to set folks in a craze
Without " ridin' sech races on Sabbath days,"
And they thought the length of the parson's prayer
Had something to do with his fatherly care.
While the truth of it was, which he afterwards
        dropped,
He didn't know what he could do when he stopped.

Of course you know how the story will end,
The prayer was finished and duly "Amen'd,"
When Tom, all dust, to the pulpit flew
And laid down the spees and the sermon too.
Then the parson preached in a timid way,
Of sinful pleasure on Sabbath-day
And he added a postscript, not in the text,
Saying that, when they were sore perplexed,
Each must decide as he chanced to feel.
And Tom chuckled: " Sundays, I'll ride my wheel."

MY STUDY CHAIR.

If the quaint old chair which has stood by my desk,
 For nearly a score of years,
Could tell all my musings, both sad and gay,
 My longings and hopes and fears,
What a tale it would tell of my youthful dreams,
 And the later years of strife!
What sombre threads it would reveal,
 In the tangled maze of life!

When the wild wind howls at my window pane,
 And the midnight fire burns low,
New-born desires and dying hopes,
 Like spectres, come and go.
I beckon the fairies down from smoke
 Or back from a goblin start,
Then nestle back in the dear old chair,
 And it soothes my restless heart.

Like a living thing it seems to me,
 When the toil of the day is done,
And it stands like a mother with loving arms,
 Outstretched toward a wayward son;
It knows how often my hidden cares
 Have found relief in tears;
It knows how the castles totter and fall
 Which a proud ambition rears.

It has found its way to my inmost heart,
  And wherever my footsteps tend,
I seem to long for its broad old arms
  As one would long for a friend.
So I hope, at last, when the Angel of Death
  Shall come from the Realms of Light,
That my dear old chair will hold me close
  Till my spirit has taken its flight.

I WONDER!

I WONDER if, under the grass-grown sod,
  The weary human heart finds rest!
If the soul, with its woes, when it flies to God,
  Leaves all its pain, in the earth's cold breast!
Or whether we feel, as we do to day,
That joy holds sorrow in hand, alway.

I wonder if, after the kiss of death,
  The love that was sweet, in days of yore,
Departs with the last, faint, fleeting breath,
  Or deeper grows than ever before!
I wonder if, there in the great Unknown,
Fond hearts grow weary when left alone!

I think of the daily life I lead,
  Its broken dreams and its fitful starts,
The hopeless hunger, the heart's sore need,
  The joy that gladdens, the wrong that parts,
And wonder whether the coming years
Will bring contentment, or toil and tears.

THE NAMELESS GUEST.

I WONDER if ever the Angel of Death
    Comes down from the great Unknown,
And soars away, on the wings of night,
    Unburdened and alone!
I wonder if ever the angels' eyes
    Are filled with pitying tears,
As they grant to the souls, unfit for flight,
    A few more weary years!

For it seems, at times, when the world is still,
    And the soft night winds are whist,
As though some spirit were hovering near,
    In folds of dream-like mist,
And I feel, though mortals are nowhere near,
    That I am not quite alone,
And, with dreary thoughts of dying and death,
    My heart grows cold as stone.

But whether 'tis death that hovers near,
    And knocks at the door of my heart,
Or whether 'tis some bright angel, come
    To be of my life a part,
I cannot tell, and I long in vain,
    The secret strange to know,
While the moments of mirth and grief and pain,
    Move on in their ceaseless flow.

And at night, when I kneel to a Higher Power
  And ask his tender care,
One yearning cry of a wayward life
  Is the burden of my prayer,
That I may bend, with willing lips,
  To kiss the chastening rod,
And learn the way, through the golden gate,
  To the great white throne of God.

A CHALLENGE.

"Good-night," he said, and he held her hand,
  In a hesitating way,
And hoped that her eyes would understand
  What his tongue refused to say.

He held her hand, and he murmured low:
  "I'm sorry to go like this.
It seems so frigidly cool, you know,
  This 'Mister' of ours, and 'Miss.'

"I thought—perchance—" and he paused to note
  If she seemed inclined to frown,
But the light in her eyes his heartstrings smote,
  As she blushingly looked down.

She spoke no word, but she picked a speck
  Of dust from his coat lapel;
So small, such a wee, little tiny fleck,
  'Twas a wonder she saw so well;

But it brought her face so very near,
  In that dim, uncertain light,
That the thought, unspoken, was made quite clear,
  And I know 'twas a sweet, "Good-night."

IMPERFECTUS.

I WONDER if ever a song was sung,
　But the singer's heart sang sweeter!
I wonder if ever a rhyme was rung,
　But the thought surpassed the meter!
I wonder if ever a sculptor wrought,
Till the cold stone echoed his ardent thought!
Or if ever a painter, with light and shade,
The dream of his inmost heart portrayed!

I wonder if ever a rose was found,
　And there might not be a fairer!
Or if ever a glittering gem was ground,
　And we dreamed not of a rarer!
Ah! never on earth do we find the best,
But it waits for us in a Land of Rest,
And a perfect thing we shall never behold,
Till we pass the portals of shining gold.

PRIORITY.

In her cozy little chamber, with her feet upon the
　　fender,
She was reading Walter Scott, the while her hus-
　　band, young and tender,
Wore a smile upon his lips that neither tongue
　　nor pen could render.

"Not one person out of twenty, with the first fond
　　lover marries,"
So she reads and o'er the sentence for a passing
　　moment tarries,
While her question, with a subtle subterfuge he
　　quickly parries.

"Was your ardent protestation unto me your first
　　confession ?"
And, "Was your beloved admission, your initial
　　concession ?"
So they questioned till it promised to become a
　　stormy session.

"Well! I married my first love, providing you
　　did," she said faintly,
"If you didn't—why—*I didn't,*" with a smile se-
　　rene and saintly,
Thus, by woman's wit, the quarrel was averted
　　very quaintly.

THE PIPES OF PAN.

BEAUTIFUL Syrinx, garland clad,
　Over the hills and dales flew she,
Goat-footed Pan pursued, like mad,
　Nothing of music then knew he;
Love, sweet love, was in his heart
And he knew no thought, from love apart.

Over the fields, through woodland bowers,
　White feet, wet with the glistening dew,
Strewing the way with fragrant flowers,
　Closely followed, the naiad flew,
Till, at last, she hid by the river bank,
Where reeds and rushes rose, rank on rank.

Baffled and breathless, here and there,
　Mad with the passion that knows no rest,
Vainly the god searched, everywhere,
　Clasping the reeds to his hairy breast,
And over their tops, as he held them fast,
The breath of his sighing swiftly passed.

And soft on his ear, a sweet sound smote,
　A sound, so mellow and deep and clear, ·
That he sought on the reeds for another note,
　To gladden and comfort his listening ear,
Till the harmony sweet that from them rose,
Like a lullaby, soothed him to calm repose.

And he only wakened to pipe again,
  And to tell his love in the new-found notes,
While the birds sought vainly to voice the strain,
  With the strength and power of their swelling
      throats,
And Syrinx, wooed from her hiding place,
Listened, with wonder upon her face.

And Echo, too, from her mountain home,
  Down o'er the valley, tripping came,
Over the stream, like a flake of foam;
  While, deep in her heart, there rose a flame,
Of love divine, for the being there,
Whose trembling music filled the air.

Ever since then, Love's sweet desire,
  Voiced in the tones of melody,
Has found the spark of a kindred fire.
  In the souls that have heard love's minstrelsy.
Love's sweet whispers, withstand who can,
Heart seeks heart, through the notes of Pan.

WHEN THE DARKNESS FALLS.

Two little hands are clasped in prayer,
  Hands like the lily leaves, so white,
Pale little lips, with a weary air,
  Murmur: " God bless my soul to night."
" Mama," the dying angel calls,
" Will papa be here, when the darkness falls ? "

Only the mother's tears reply:
  Truth is, at times, too sad to tell;
Maddened with grief, she hears that cry,
  Asking for one in a prison cell.
" Mama," the dying baby calls,
" Will papa be here, when the darkness falls ? "

Slower and feebler each fleeting breath,
  Whiter the face that is pure as snow,
Swifter the flight of the angel Death,
  Deeper the depth of the mother's woe.
" Mama," again her darling calls,
" Will papa be here, when the darkness falls ? "

Just as the daylight fades away,
  And the last faint ray sinks out of sight,
Sweet lips wearily strive to pray;
  But the soul takes wing, with the waning light.
Baby is dead, but from Heaven still calls:
" Papa, dear, come when the darkness falls."

AT SUNRISE.

Over the green grass, wet with dew,
Lightly tripping, a maiden flew,
Eyes alight with the gleam of love,
And the golden sunlight fair above.

Now she stops, and o'er the wall,
    Dainty fingers and nimble feet
Cautiously climb, where wild vines crawl,
    Plucking a nosegay, fresh and sweet.
" If you wouldn't be plucked from your mossy bed,
You never should be so sweet," she said.

Over the fields, with a sturdy stride,
A yeoman stepped to the maiden's side,
And over the cheeks, that flushed so red,
With a tender smile, he bent his head,

And his arm stole gently 'round her there,
    While the nosegay fell to the ground, unseen,
And the song-birds warbled a sprightlier air,
    For he kissed her a hundred times, I ween.
" If you'd keep your kisses, dear lips so red,
You never should be so sweet," he said.

LET SILENCE FALL.

LET silence fall across the past,
  Its fitful moods of storm and rain,
  Its weary hours of jealous pain,
Let never heart or speech recall,
  If memory needs must break the spell,
  Remember—that I loved you well,
And o'er the rest—let silence fall.

Let silence fall between our lives,
  The one, sunlit, with youthful dreams,
  Flushed, with the future's hopeful gleams
And held in proud ambition's thrall,
  The other, worn with anxious tears,
  And tired grown, with gathering years,
Between them now—let silence fall.

And let us part, as those who love,
  Are parted, by the hand of Death,
  And one stands, hushed, with reverent breath,
Gazing on funeral bier and pall,
  But ere we close the coffin lid,
  Let bitter memories all be hid,
And o'er the grave—let silence fall.

A CHOICE.

'Tis weak to love, if all the world
    Is fickle, false and vain;
'Tis sweet to love, though all the world
    Knows well that love is pain.

'Tis vain to love, if love must change,
    And fill the eyes with tears;
'Tis wise to love, e'en though love range,
    And rack the heart with fears.

'Tis vain, 'tis wise, 'tis weak, 'tis strong,
    We know not what to do,
We only know the days are long,
    When loving words are few.

To love is pain, ah! yes, 'tis true,
    And ever so 'twill be,
But not to love and not to woo,
    Is greater all agree.

So give me love, and let me find
    The sweeter, lesser woe;
Love, fillet-bound, shall lead me blind
    Wherever he may go.

THE RING.

A BAND of burnished gold
My fingers gently hold,
And through the magic circle of its rim,
    Before my dreaming eyes
    A thousand memories rise
And fill my soul with longing, vague and dim.

    I seem to see the gate,
    At which I used to wait,
For her who gave to me this token sweet;
    I feel a tender thrill
    That calls to mind the hill,
Where hours, like moments, fled on pinions fleet.

    The form of youthful grace,
    The smiling tender face,
Is near me still, in spirit, though the years
    Have slowly come and fled
    And cherished hopes lie dead
Along my way, too thickly strewn for tears.

    Oh! little band of gold!
    A wealth of joy untold
Your shining circle conjures to my mind,
    And will. until my breath
    Shall meet the kiss of death,
And all the pain of earth is left behind.

AN OLD SKULL.

Under a tree, in a grassy glade,
Delved I deep, with a well-worn spade,
And there, half-hid in the soil, I saw
A row of teeth and a lower jaw,
    'Twas a skull all gray and grinning.

With a bit of glass I scraped it clean,
'Twas the first of its kind I had ever seen,
So I fixed the jaw with a piece of twine,
Hung the skull on a climbing vine,
    And said, with an accent winning:

" I say, old skull, you've a happy face,
I thought that the grave was a dismal place,
I'll wager a hat that when on earth
You hadn't that permanent look of mirth,
    And frowned as you went about sinning.

Confess if you're happier now than then,
And I'll put you back in the earth again,
Refuse and your future shall surely be
In the dusty den of an old M.D.
    The old skull kept on grinning.

A CHRISTMAS STORY.

I.

I PASSED the door of a house last night,
  Where a rich man lives, in a princely way,
And asleep on the steps, lay a man, half clad,
  Benumbed with the cold, and with sorrow gray;
The mansions grand were ablaze with light.
  I could hear the tread of the dancers' feet,
But mourning bands swung to and fro,
  From the one dark door on the brilliant street.

II.

'Twas a pitiful story I listened to,
  Of a ruined home and a blighted life,
For the woman, dead, in the rich man's house,
  Had been the sleeper's misguided wife.
I touched his shoulder and said: "See here,
  There's a storm, in the sky there, off to the west,
Just gather yourself together, my man,
  This isn't a very good place to rest.

III.

" These stones are hard that you're lying on.
  Hard as the hearts of the men you meet.
There are beds to be had, for a dime or so,
  Which are better than stones in the open street.
I haven't an over supply myself,
  Of the cash you seem to sadly need.
But here's for a lodging and breakfast, man,
  I wish it were more; take the will for the deed."

IV.

"That's the first kind word that my ears have
    heard,
    For a month or more," the man replied.
" I'm only the wreck of the man I was,
    But a kind word rouses the old-time pride,
I don't owe a dollar, in this wide world,
    Not a single cent to a living man,
I've worked like a slave, to find success;
    But I've finished, I've striven all I can.

V.

" I've seen bright days, when my purse was lined
    With bills and silver and yellow gold,
I've known the joys of a happy home,
    And alas! I've seen the wolf in the fold ;
A wolf, that came in a friend's disguise,
    And stole the love of a gentle wife,
Robbed me of happiness, home and hope,
    Snatched all the joy and light from my life.

VI.

" She didn't love him. She loved me well,
    Till the time when poverty's curse was mine;
Ill fortune had followed my first success,
    And she—well—her tastes were always fine;
So, when the tempter spread out his wealth,
    And pictured the comforts it would buy,
There was little need of persuasion then,
    He found her more than ready to fly.

VII.

"Did we have a child? Oh! yes, a boy;
  A bright-eyed, happy-hearted lad,
He was eight years old when I saw him last,
  And he stuck to his father, through good and
    bad.
But I lost him too; I was out one day,
  Hunting employment, from store to store,
The rent was due and I knew right well
  If I asked for time, I could get no more.

VIII.

"So I hurried about, in the broiling sun,
  Heartsick and footsore and weary—well—
I only remember that all turned black
  And I sank, in a sort of a fainting spell.
'Twas a week before I knew where I was,
  In the ward of a hospital, cool and clean,
And when I was better, my boy was gone,
  For days, not a sign of him had been seen.

IX.

"I thought she took him, or better still,
  Perhaps God took him, in time to save
His bright young eyes from the dreary sight
  Of a father, dead, in an unmarked grave:
I'm not a drunkard, sir; look at my face,
  It isn't bloated, it's pale and thin
And worn with the failures I've met, so long,
  And saddened from losing, where others win.

X.

" But give me the coin, sir: your card as well,
  Some day, if Fortune should smile again,
I'll pay it back and will walk, perhaps,
  With my head erect, like other men,
For I'll try once more and if failure comes,
  I know of a refuge from all this strife,
Where many a soul finds rest and peace,
  Who has broken down on the road of life.

XI.

" There's a news-boy yonder. Perhaps you'll find,
  In one of his papers, a place for me;
Just glance one over and read me, sir,
  A few of the likeliest ' wants' you see."
I called to the boy : " Look here, my lad,
  Will you lend us a paper a second or two ? "
He laughed as he answered : " There ain't any law
  Against my *sellin'* a paper to you."

XII.

At the sound of his voice, the old man stared,
  And put out his hand in a groping way,
Then passed it over his forehead, bare,
  As though his senses had gone astray.
" What's wrong ? " I questioned, but still he stood,
  And murmured a name, but he did not stir,
Then he said, as he looked at the rich man's
    door,
  " That voice, somehow, led me to think of her.

XIII.

" Supposing—but no—it's a foolish thought,
    There's no such fortune in store for me."
But I called the boy quickly, " This way, my lad,
    Turn your face to the light, where I can see.
I want you to tell me your name," I said.
        He answered me smiling: " It's ' Deacon   or
            ' Fool,'
They call me the first 'cause I never swear,
    And belong to a class in the Sunday-school.

XIV.

" They call me the other, just 'cause, sometimes,
    When some o' the boys, that ain't real bright,
Get stuck on their papers, I buy 'em out
    And sell 'em by stayin' out late at night.
That's why I'm a-workin' as late as this."
    " But what is your real name," I asked of him.
Before he could answer, the man spoke up,
    And his voice was husky, his eyes were dim.

XV.

" Can you remember, four years ago,
    A father who loved you, and every night,
Read stories to please you and heard your prayers,
    And made you a monster, big, paper kite ? "
" Why, yes ! " said the boy, " and I asked him once,
    If I had a mother, way up in Heaven.
He told me, ' No,' but I heard him say,
    " I wonder if such ones are ever forgiven.' "

XVI.

The poor man staggered, as from a blow,
  For the bands of crape he could plainly see.
" Not a word to the boy, to night," he said,
  " He wouldn't be proud of a man like me;
He is mine once more, and I feel, somehow,
  I can work and strive like other men;
I'll watch him and guard him until, with pride,
  His lips shall breathe the word ' father ' again.

XVII.

" You'll see me, to-morrow, a different man,
  It's a pleasure to work for a noble son;
Come, boy, let's go to a lodging house;
  Good night, sir.   God bless you for what you've
    done."
      *   *   *   *   *   *   *   *
To-night, I met them, a happy pair,
  Well dressed and planning a future bright,
For both had a purpose and work to do,
  Beginning, they told me, with Christmas night.

XVIII.

From the church, near by, an anthem rose,
  " Glad tidings, and peace, on earth good-will,"
I heard him murmur, with trembling voice,
  "And the prayers of thy servant, O Lord! fulfil;"
'Twas an earnest prayer, and I said "Amen,"
  I knew he had prayed for the boy at his side.
" Good night; good fortune attend you," I said,
  "And keep the good cheer of your Christmas-
    tide."

SPRING SONG.

Oh! I am a fairy, in garments green,
  My wings are as light as air,
My slippers are dainty as e'er were seen,
  And a magical wand I bear.
      I hide in the nooks,
      By the frozen brooks,
And coax them to break old Winter's chains ;
      And his old bones crack,
      As I drive him back,
With his blustering winds, to his own domains.

I tease him with showers, by day and night,
  Until he is glad to go;
I laugh when he clutches in wild affright
  His glistening robe of snow;
      I lovingly peep
      At the flowers asleep,
And kiss them to life when the blue birds sing.
      I am light and gay
      Through the live-long day,
And the happiest child of the year is Spring.

THE RABBI AND THE PRINCE.

VERSIFIED FROM THE TALMUD.

A MONARCH sat in serious thought, alone,
But little reck'd he of his robe and throne;
Naught valuing the glory of control,
He sought to solve the future of his soul.
" Why should I bow the proud, imperious knee,
To mighty powers no mortal eye can see ? "
So mused he long and turned this question o'er,
Then, with impatient tread, he paced the floor,
Till maddened by conflicting trains of thought
And speculations vague, which came to naught,
With feverish haste he clutched a tasseled cord
As desperate hands, in battle, clutch a sword.
" Summon Jehoshua," the monarch cried.
The white-haired Rabbi soon was at his side.

   *   *   *   *   *   *

" I bow no more to powers I cannot see;
Thy faith and learning shall be naught to me,
Unless, before the setting of the sun,
Mine eyes behold the uncreated one."

   *   *   *   *   *   *

The Rabbi led him to the open air.
The oriental sun with furious glare
Sent down its rays, like beams of molten gold.
The aged teacher, pointing, said: " Behold."

"I cannot," said the Prince, "my dazzled eyes
Refuse their service, turned upon the skies."

   *   *   *   *   *   *

"Son of the dust," the Rabbi gently said
And bowed, with reverence, his hoary head,
"This one creation, thou canst not behold,
Though by thy lofty state and pride made bold.
How canst thou then behold the God of Light,
Before whose face these sunbeams are as night?
Thine eyes before this trifling labor fall,
Canst gaze on Him who hath created all?
Son of the dust, repentance can atone;
Return and worship God, who rules alone."

THE GREEN-ROOM GLASS.

I'm only a battered old green-room glass,
  But I've done my duty for many years,
Telling a story to all who pass,
  Of joy and sadness, of smiles and tears.

Ah! but my tale is a varied one,
  For I have seen fond hopes decay;
Bright, happy lives that were just begun
  Saddened by sorrow, grow old and gray.

I have seen ladies of wealth and fame,
  Wearing the rags of a pauper's fate;
I have seen others, without a name,
  Clad in the robes of royal state.

Children that prattled, before my face,
  I have seen grow into great renown;
Others, alas! have met deep disgrace,
  Scorned by companions and shunned by the town.

Ah! but 'tis sad when I see a face
  Wrinkled and pale, with the flight of years,
Which I once knew so full of grace;
  Radiant smiles, where now are tears.

Vassal and master, matron and maid,
  Look at me, smile at me, just the same,
Each in a transient garb arranged,
  Seeking the vanishing bubble—Fame.

Often I hear them cry out in pain,
   Often I long to bend down and bless,
Weary, worn mortals, that strive in vain,
   Failing where others have found success.

Never from me is a thing concealed—
   Here, before me, they must all confess;
Standing alone and with hearts revealed,
   Donning their smiles as they don their dress.

Oh! to be free from this gas-lit place,
   Brightened again by the flowers and grass!
Oh! for Reality's honest face—
   Weary of sham is the green-room glass.

A SEA SONG.

I LOVE the sea! I love the sea!
And the spray from its waves comes kissing me,
    As I stand on the shore,
    When the flood tides roar
And the white caps dance right merrily.

The dear, old waves, from the coral caves,
And the sunny strands that the water laves,
    Come close to my feet,
    With legends sweet,
Of the mighty ocean's domes and naves.

The whole day long, they croon a song,
And the red-lipped shells the sound prolong,
    Of a loved one dear,
    Who is hastening here,
On a ship that is swift and staunch and strong.

THE QUIET HOUR.

At sunset, out across the hills,
　I rode into the dying day;
The brooks sang low, with tender trills,
　The birds were silent on my way.

The crickets chirped in monotone;
　The bees were sleeping on the hill;
The wind swept by with solemn moan;
　My heart grew sad, my voice was still.

Yet, in my breast sweet thoughts were born,
　Unmixed with aught of earth's alloy,
And words were faltering and out-worn,
　That sought to voice my silent joy.

The quiet hour of eventide
　Subdues man's stormy soul within,
And pure thoughts through his musings glide
　Without a trace of soil or sin.

But with the joy of high-born thought,
　There is a lingering touch of pain,
A yearning, with sweet suffering fraught,
　When utterance strives, and strives in vain.

But while the sombre shadows slept
　Upon the hills and o'er the vales,
Between the trees the moonbeams crept,
　And swift illumed the quiet dales.

The silver moonlight, sifting through
  The leaves and branches of the trees,
On wings of light, around me flew,
  And mingled with the shifting breeze.

Like mist at morn, sad thoughts took flight,
  The wide world opened like a scroll,
And ere the day had turned to night
  Delight alone filled all my soul.

IN NO-MAN'S-LAND.

Two shapes were walking, on the strand,
One starlit night, in no-man's land,

Two shapes that, during mortal life,
Gave hate for hate, in deadly strife.

They met. Swift forth their falchions flew;
Each pierced the other, through and through;

Yet neither fell. Again they strove
For mastery, and madly drove

To right and left their falchions bright;
Nor sound, nor cry profaned the night.

Through corselet, casque and visor too,
As through the air their swift blades flew;

Until amazed, they stood aghast,
And on the sands their weapons cast.

Then laughed they both at mortal strife,
The passing dream of earthly life.

And clasping each the other's hand,
They walk the shades of no-man's land.

SEPTEMBER REVERY.

I CAN'T seem to realize, fully,
    How quickly the season has flown;
I've scarce had a day through the summer,
    To rest and to be quite alone.
I've been yachting and driving and bathing,
    I know every horse on the track;
And I've planned out a beautiful future;
    I'm engaged to be married to Jack.

From the first of July to September,
    Is not a long courtship I know;
But then, if we wait until Christmas,
    'Twill be half a twelvemonth, and so,
After telling Jack " Yes," on an impulse,
    I couldn't somehow take it back;
And he says we can court all our lifetime,
    So I'm to be married to Jack.

He hasn't a very large fortune,
    But he's handsome and brimful of life,
And he says that his prospects will brighten
    With me for his own little wife.
How little I dreamed when I came here,
    How settled and staid I'd go back!
Not caring for flirting and dancing,
    For I'm to be married to Jack.

I thought, at the first of the season,
    Of titles and money and style;
But the charm which they hold is but trifling,
    When I think of his bright, tender smile.
Ah, me! when a girl loves her lover,
    Of happiness there is no lack;
My heart is as light as a feather,
    I'm engaged to be married to Jack.

THE LAST GLADIATORIAL COMBAT.

THE scene of conflict was the Libyan plain;
Honorius, Emperor, sat in proud disdain,
Upon his blazoned throne, half lost in thought,
For death that raged below him caring naught.

The sands lay glistening in the torrid sun,
Blood-red, where many a brave life-tide had run,
And ere the day crept down the glowing west,
A hundred souls had found eternal rest.

With flashing swords uplifted in their hands,
Two gladiators met upon the sands,
Firm friends and fast, yet mortal was their strife,
For one, to live, must take the other's life.

Their glances met for one swift, fleeting breath,
And read this thought: " No wounds, but speedy
          death."
With valorous swords, they fought both long and
          well,
Till one, with broken sword-blade, tripped and fell.

The hoarse-voiced rabble shouted loudly: " Kill! "
The victor turned to learn the Emperor's will,
His pleading eyes beseeching him to spare,
But, lost in thought, the monarch gazed in air.

"Kill! Kill!" the rabble shouted, growing bold,
The bright blade gleamed, when loud a voice cried
    "Hold!"
And swift, across those reeking Libyan sands,
A white-haired monk rushed forth, with lifted
    hands.

The multitude, in silence, stood aghast;
The monarch from his reverie roused, at last,
When brave Telemachus, devoid of fear,
Proclaimed aloud: "The wrath of God is near.

"Four hundred years the Word of God hath
    taught:
'Thou shalt not kill,' and shall it go for naught!
Shall kings a price of human bloodshed pay,
To make, for savage men, a holiday?

"Honorius, Emperor though thou art, beware!
Nor king, nor slave, the wrath of God can dare."
Swift o'er the arena twenty warriors trod,
And twenty swords struck down the man of God.

But through his death his words became a power
To move Honorius, every day and hour,
Until, at last, the monarch's royal hand,
Sent forth an edict o'er the Libyan land.

"Thou shalt not kill. The Word of God revere,
Thy captive slaves release from bondage drear."
Small need of praise from mortal tongue or pen
For him who died to save his fellow-men.

A DREAM OF SUMMER.

OUT through the summer's golden glow,
  Across the land, into the west,
I rode at sunset, sad and slow,
  Where the end of the rainbow sinks to rest,
Out toward the realms of the setting sun,
As the night came down and the day was done.

The insects hummed a lullaby,
  In cozy homes of folded leaves;
The birds had ceased to chirp on high,
  Within their nests, beneath the eaves;
The nodding flowers, along the way,
Seemed bowing low, to slumber's sway.

Adown the path, where arching trees,
  Clasped hands and kissed, with lips of leaves,
I drank the burden of the breeze,
  The scent of flowers and garnered sheaves,
And, over all, the lingering light
Of sunbeams and the stars of night.

Alas! these dreams of summers past
  Will drift into our drowsy hours;
Too sweet, too Heavenly high to last,
  But laden with the breath of flowers;
Within, bright thoughts and memories sweet,
Without, the snow and blinding sleet.

ON THE WAY.

Soft shadows fall along the wall,
  That girts the roadway where I run,
The waning light foretells the night
  And swift pursues the retreating sun,
I see afar a twinkling star—
  The herald of a million more,
The great waves creep, as half asleep,
  Along the distant, sandy shore.

The world is still, and yet a thrill
  Of joy intense pervades my soul,
While Nature seems to be in dreams,
  As down the gentle slope I roll:
The rifted clouds that drift in crowds
  Along the far horizon's rim,
Reflect the rays of distant days'
  Last lingering sunlight faint and dim.

A sweet wild rose unnoticed grows,
  Half-hidden in the long, strong grass;
Sweet thoughts arise of love-lit eyes—
  I lean and clutch it as I pass.
My love will wear within her hair
  This sweet memento of the hour;
I shall forget the dream; but yet
  My life has felt its subtle power.

MISERRIMUS.

THE down of thistles, swaying on the breeze,
An autumn leaflet, falling from the trees,
A bit of drift-wood, floating down the stream,
A subtle fancy, passing in a dream,
Thus pass our days, and like a deep-drawn sigh
The noblest life but lives to say " Good-by."

O Life! O Death! We know not which is best,
The day of toil or night's unending rest;
Long vistas in our future we unfold
And find, at last, a dream that soon is told.
Happy the man whose life is boundless love
For that which waits us, in the realms above.

Will that time come, when hearts will cease to beat
O'er earthly joys? when Love's first kisses sweet
Give no delight?   Ah! then and then alone,
Poor weary hearts will cease to sigh and moan;
Plunge as we will into the world's wild din,
We cannot drown the heartache hid within.

PASSING CLOUDS.

IN leafy dales, where song-birds sing
  Their notes of joy the whole day through,
'Tis sweet to watch the clouds that float
  Across the broad expanse of blue,
And with each cloud let bright hopes rise
    That comfort you.

What though each cloud is not like snow
  Fringed round with golden beams of light,
To know and feel the sunlit day
  We needs must pass through shades of night,
And something comes, in each dark day,
    That comforts you.

Then let bright clouds cheer up your heart,
  And put sad, dreary thoughts to flight,
And let the dark ones cheer you too,
  They make the bright ones seem more bright,
Thus, life is made one long, sweet dream
    That comforts you.

THE TIGER AND THE TWIN;

A SEQUEL TO THE LADY OR THE TIGER.

For six long years the patient literary public of two continents has been treading the maze of ethical discussion and pondering over the intricacies of psychic formulæ, endeavoring to determine by the analogy of mental processes whether a lady or a tiger emerged from a certain, mysterious door, toward which the heroine of the thrilling tale had made a lightning-like gesture.

It will be remembered by those who read the story calmly and seriously, as was befitting such a narrative, that the courtier who had dared to love the daughter of his King, entered the arena, at a given signal, and traversed half the distance, in the direction of the twin doors, opposite the throne of the semi-barbaric imperial presence.

He then turned, as was the custom, to make his obeisance, but instead of doing so, fixed his eyes upon the trembling princess, believing that her love for him had led her to discover behind which door crouched a hungry tiger, ready and willing to devour him and behind which stood a waiting and blushing maiden, more than ready and willing to wed him.

As was stated in the narrative, the punishments for guilt and the rewards of innocence were comparatively instantaneous; indeed, so swift was the administration of the decree, that before the prisoner could fully realize his mistake he would be located in the tiger's interior, while, on the other hand, his reward was characterized by the same remarkable celerity, for the instant the waiting maiden stepped into the arena, from a door opposite, a priest with attendants entered to perform the wedding ceremony, and the children treading epithalamic measures circled around the semistunned bridegroom so hilariously that he could scarcely collect his senses sufficiently to note how exceedingly epithalamic the measures were. It is not to be wondered at, considering the trepidation with which he had looked forward to this critical juncture, that his gaze, for the instant, was more penetrating than tender, and it may have been this lack of tenderness which aroused, in the mind of the princess, a question as to whether the courtier might not be more than content to win existence by a fortunate choice, regardless of the maiden's identity.

Especial care had always been exercised in the selection of maidens, particular attention having been paid to the appropriateness of the possible union.

His manner betrayed nothing but severe cogitation as to the justice of turning over to mere chance the decreeing of sudden death or equally sudden marriage. In his hours of imprisonment, while the princess had been impairing her beauty by the violence of her emotions, he had been

speculating on the probabilities in favor of his
choosing the door to the left. Through many
trifling gifts, but more through his grace and
courtliness, he had managed to win the sympathies
of his jailor, and from him had learned that out of
forty-seven judgments, in which the semi-barbaric
King had resorted to the problematic justice of
the lady and the tiger, thirty-two had chosen the
door to the right and been devoured. Certain
subjects had secretly entertained a suspicion that
even the King's rectitude was not proof against
the temptation to put a tiger behind both doors,
when a grievance of his own was to be adjudicated,
but nothing could be ocularly demonstrated to
that effect, since thirty-two, after making a choice,
were practically incapable of making another, and
fifteen were amply content to remain devoid of
meddling curiosity as to what the other door might
conceal. He also learned that, at the last five trials,
the tiger had been concealed behind the door to
the right.

By a system of equalization, or law of probabilities, he reasoned that the usual sequence of varia-
tion pointed toward the door on the left and he
had determined upon making that choice.

Knowing the intensity of feeling which must
have swayed the princess at the moment their eyes
met, the doubt which was born in his breast, as to
her willingness to see him in the arms of another,
for the time usurped supremacy over all his mental functions.

The impetuosity of her gesture might betoken

the entirety of an affection which controlled every
fibre of her being, lending all its force to the mus-
cular dictations, or it might betray the eagerness
of a sudden resolve to endure one terrible moment
rather than the years of slow torture which his
marriage with another would necessarily involve,
should she prove unable to outgrow the psychic
influence with which the courtier had permeated
her entire existence.

For an instant, only, he wavered between the
dictations of his law of probabilities and the swift
mandate of the princess. Even though she should
misdirect him, he could die feeling that a devotion, sufficiently vigorous to suggest such extreme
measures, must contain the elements requisite for
continuance beyond an earthly career, and as the
days of earth constituted merely a transition period
to that state where the aspirations of the soul tran-
scend the corporeal attributes, he believed it ad-
visable to follow the suggestion which his eye
alone had recognized. With this thought in mind,
he strode boldly to the door on the right and fling-
ing it back upon its well-oiled hinges beheld—A
TIGER.

The natural instinct of self-preservation caused
him to start back, and immediately following this
mental shock came the realization that the princess had sent him to his death, but while these
bewildering emotions were warring in his breast,
something in the demeanor of the tiger caused
him to observe more closely the apparent inten-
tions of the beast. The customary spring from

the conchant to the rampant attitude had been lacking; the savage roar which had been in the habit of echoing and re-echoing through the caverns and corridors of the amphitheatre was also missing. The whole bearing of the animal seemed amicable to an amazing degree.

One swift, searching glance gave to the courtier the key to the situation, and whispering an Arabic name, under his breath, to the tiger, the animal, docile as a kitten, came to him and licked his hand. Another word, again in the Arabic tongue, and the tiger sprawled at his feet, permitting him to place his foot upon his neck.

Long years before, in the wilds of an Arabian jungle, a twin brother of the courtier had captured this same tiger, and as playmates they had grown up together. Doubtless the keeper in the doorway beyond was the twin, disguised. The courtier saluted the King, while the multitude rent the air with shouts. Some rejoiced that one so brave and fair and young should escape so terrible a fate, while many were maddened by the disappointment of beholding neither a tragedy nor a comedy, but a spectacle in which the component parts of both had been strangely commingled.

It was evident that the twin had brought about his brother's deliverance, but surely through the power and influence of the princess, and this proof of her fidelity flushed his cheek with joy.

The semi-barbaric King was tossed hither and thither on the waves of indecision. His method of administering justice had miscarried. That

which had heretofore been determinate and final,
now became uncertain and unsatisfying.

The courtier had chosen the door which be-
tokened guilt, yet guilt had not met with punishment. Had he chosen the other door and had the
maiden refused to marry, he could not have been
more surprised than was he at the amicability of
the tiger. He had ordered the fiercest beast at-
tainable, and had specified that he should fast for
three days prior to the exhibition. Hitherto ab-
solutely absolute in his authority, the semi-barbaric
King allowed the semi in his character to outmas-
ter the barbaric and resolved that the situation
was one which demanded the deliberations and
counsel of other minds. Summoning his followers,
he chose, from their number, those in whom he
believed intuitive perception had reached its ripest
perfection, ordered the courtier to be once more
incarcerated and led the way to the council chamber.

In his agitation over the upheaval of his pet
theory of poetic justice, the King neglected to
appoint a special guardian for the prisoner, and
the princess being older than her younger brother,
seized the opportunity of appointing a man whose
trustworthiness in underhand matters was pro-
verbial.

The arguments of the counsellors lasted far into
the night, and the final verdict was that if the
tiger had been tampered with and it should be
proven by careful examination that he had been
overfed rather than starved, the courtier should be

compelled to pass through the ordeal of judicial choice again.

If, on the contrary, the orders of the King had been obeyed, the comeliest maiden in the kingdom should be given him to wed.

Shortly after sunrise on the following morning the ringing of bells and the voices of the heralds gave notice to the patrons of the arena that some one of their number had ignored the imperial mandate and fed the tiger, and that on the following day the fiercest beast ever placed in captivity would be behind one of the twin doors, while behind the other should stand a maiden, who was beloved, as all the kingdom knew, by the younger brother of the princess and who had long since showed by word and sign that the prospectively imperial affection was not distasteful to her.

The trustworthiness of the guardian selected by the princess remained intact, and by a simple process of secret communication it was arranged that the young prince should disguise himself as the courtier and choosing the door to the left meet the woman of his choice and be there and then wed according to the usual rites. Being the daughter of a semi-barbaric father, of course the princess possessed certain component parts which were barbaric in character, yet it was not entirely the possession of these elements which brought about the stirring incidents of the second trial. At the usual signal, a youth, to all appearance the courtier, advanced to the centre of the arena, saluted the King and stepping lightly to the door on the left, threw it open and clasped close to his breast the woman he adored.

From another door a priest with attendants appeared and the marriage was solemnized, after which the children strewed flowers to the foot of the throne upon which sat the King, wrapped in a cloud of thought as to whether or not some subtle power beyond his control watched over and protected the youth who had thus miraculously escaped a second time.

As the wedding procession drew near, however, the sharp eyes of the King pierced the disguise of the prince and recognized the son. Semi-barbaric rage, more than any other, resorts to excess when roused to its full completeness, and so it came about that the King, attired in his robes of state, rushed to the centre of the arena and uttered an oath of vengeance upon all who had conspired to overthrow his judicial system.

Knowing that the prince was lacking in courage and doubting if there had been any chance in his choice of doors, the King believed that no tiger had been provided. Impelled by this idea and fatally eager to determine the fact, he flew to the door on the right, flung it open and was speedily devoured. The prince, thus becoming king, elevated the courtier to a rank befitting his valor and the depth of his devotion, and his marriage with the princess was consummated with as much hilarity as was consistent, considering the proximity and peculiarity of a demise so eminently semi-barbaric.

Thus, after six years of anxious solicitude, the
great reading public learns, that in the impartial
justification of this single instance, not only did
the lady emerge from the hidden recesses but the
lady and two tigers, one tame and the other not so
much so.

IN LONDON TOWER.

[In an old worm-eaten chest, the property of a lodger named William Willston, who died in a London tenement, was found the MS. of the tale which follows.

Whether it is a true recital of an unrecorded escape, or whether it is from the imagination of some partially insane person, will probably never be known, as all traces are lost beyond the time of Berthold Willston, an inn-keeper and great grandfather of the deceased lodger. To him the possession of the old chest has been traced. The condition of the MS., the texture of the paper, the appearance of the ink, which is but dimly seen on the paper, and the mention of the broken sword with the jeweled hilt, lead to the belief that the MS. is certainly of great age, and that it belongs to the period when such imprisonments were not unusual.]

I, William Worthington, believing that I am about to die, pray to Heaven for strength to tell a tale of wrong and suffering. I know not the year in which I am living. I dare not ask. I only pray for strength to finish, for my wife and children, if they still live, the story of my woes. The shock of freedom upon my broken constitution is proving too great, and I feel that death is near. I was a warder in the Tower of London. For twenty years I had been faithful to my trust, and had lived according to the dictations of an honest heart.

Every prisoner placed under my surveillance for twenty years had been tried, judged and sentenced by my inner consciousness; and as my intuitions led me, so were they treated, though I never violated a law. It is within the power of a warder to add greatly to a prisoner's comfort and welfare, though he may grant no illegal freedom. Books, pipes, writing materials and games were speedily forthcoming for those whom I believed more sinned against than sinning.

It mattered not to me whether the accused was a duke or an earl in the turret chambers, or a peasant in the dungeon.

By this inner tribunal of my own, I judged that the Duke of Elton had been a traitor to his king, and from my hands he received no favors beyond the requirements of the law.

I little dreamed that so great a personage would wreak vengeance upon a vassal, so far below him, yet his hirelings gave oath, months after his release, that during a time when the utmost watchfulness had been enjoined upon the warders I was found asleep at my post. During that critical period the penalty was death.

That very day I had walked far into the suburbs of London, on leave of absence to visit my family, and had returned to take my usual watch from nine at night until nine on the following morning.

I was weary and travel-stained, which told against me, but as there is a just God in Heaven, I did not sleep on my post, neither that night nor any night during my years of service. A warder had once slept and allowed the escape of political prisoners. He was accused of complicity, and the death penalty had been instituted.

I could prove nothing. I had paced the corridors through the night, but the prisoners had slept and could say nothing to save me.

Two men claimed to have passed through the corridor as the clock struck twelve, and upon their oaths affirmed that I was sleeping. If they entered the corridor at all, it was while I was at the further end, and they must have left it before my return. In vain I protested my innocence. The friends of the Duke of Elton were in favor, and my doom seemed inevitable.

I had been foully dealt with, and during a short recess I bethought me of foul means for escape.

I had a staunch friend in the tower, a fellow-warder. I would risk everything and trust to him. The infinite patience and kindness of a mother's love had taught me to write, and I carelessly toyed with the materials at hand. Stealthily writing a word or two now and then, without detection, at last it was finished, no whit too soon, for the opportunity came at once to slip into the warder's hand, unseen, this writing:

"Haste to the clock, outside the wall. Cut, with a saw, a thirteenth notch, after the twelve, in the striking wheel, and save the life of WILLIAM WORTHINGTON."

With this paper crumpled in his hand, he gave his evidence, which availed me naught, save to prove that I was at my post before eleven o'clock, and that the usual greetings were exchanged.

As he passed out he gave me a searching look, but its meaning I could not divine. I could not tell his bearing toward me. If I were removed, my place would become his, and I was a little above him. Would he risk imprisonment for himself to save me?

Midnight alone could answer.

For the last time I was asked if I had aught to say, and, as though under the influence of a sudden recollection, I said:

"These men claim that the clock struck twelve while I was sleeping. At twelve o'clock I was awake, in proof of which know this: The great clock needs repairing, for at twelve in the night I counted thirteen strokes of the bell. It will probably do so again to-night. Wait and see."

"Oh, the horror of those hours of waiting! Three! Four! Five! Six o'clock, and for the first time in twenty years, save for my holidays, I was not in my place. Seven! Eight! Nine! and still the hours dragged on, wearily, when I bethought me of the all-absorbing issue, but much too swiftly if that wooden wheel was untouched.

Ten and eleven o'clock struck. Then came the longest hour of my life. Days and weeks seemed to pass, and all the actions of my life in slow procession trooped before me. I longed for midnight, and yet dreaded to know what fate it held in store for me.

Had he deserted me in my darkest hour? Would he strive for me and for justice to an innocent man?

"Boom!"—came the first stroke from the great bell. With breathless lips I counted the strokes, at each one pressing a finger into the palm of my

hand so hard that the nail pierced the skin.
Four fingers had thus closed on the right hand,
and over them the thumb, recording the fifth
stroke. Four more on the left hand, and slowly
over them closed the thumb, like a band of steel.
Eleven! The hands flew open and I started forward, listening, trembling, praying. Twelve! I
could feel the very vibrations of the bell beating
against my temples as the iron tongue struck the
side. Thirteen! Thank God! He had befriended
me in my hour of need. I fell fainting to the
floor, and from sheer exhaustion slept till daybreak.

I believe that the judges would have reinstated
me, could they have been allowed to use their own
discretion, but powerful enemies were at work
against me and the freshly-sawed slot in the striking wheel of the clock was discovered, and I was
again summoned for further trial. The guards
swore that no person had access to me after my
arrest and thus left a doubt in their minds. This
doubt caused them to modify the death sentence
to solitary confinement in the lower dungeon of
the tower. What a modification! To bid farewell
forever to wife and children; never to look again
upon the fields and the grass, the trees and the
birds and the beautiful sunshine; to live, like a
rat, in a dark and dismal hole, until, like a rat, I
could see the dampness oozing out between the
stones of my cell as well by night as by day.

Better death than that; better to know that one
swift stroke would end all earthly suffering and
that revengeful enmity could never more assail me.

But prisoners had escaped from this very tower before and why not again? I would wait and hope and strive; wait for the unfolding of the future's mysterious problems, hope for those almost miraculous changes that sometimes shift the power of a sovereign in the twinkling of an eye; strive, if I could; but what is the strife of one close kept within a rock-bound cell! So in my solitude I sat for hours, brooding upon my condition. Then came the desire to know my surroundings more intimately. How well I know each stone, each line and fissure!

I could press my hands upon a bed of yielding clay and reproduce the walls of my cell so accurately that a mould of one would fit the other so closely a stream of water could not trickle through between them. Each stone I hate, save those I moved aside and broke against each other to use as implements of toil.

My cell was nine feet high, five feet broad and ten feet deep. Two bars of iron inserted in the solid rock supported four boards six inches wide and two inches in thickness, which, with a coarse blanket and a sack of straw composed my bed. Along the outer edge of the planks was fastened another one, extending one and a half inches above the edge; a three-legged stool and a billet of wood to place beneath the sack of straw for a pillow, completed the equipment of the cell.

Through an opening in the heavy door I could see damp walls and other heavy doors. Through this opening, at irregular intervals, was thrust a loaf of bread and a jug of water, and at times a piece of meat would be left, without a word, upon the shelf at the opening. Many a time have I raised the jug to dash it against the stones and with the ragged edge sever an artery, but each time the faint spark of hope has stayed my hand. During the first few days, thoughts of the injustice that had been done to me and the strangeness of my surroundings gave food for reflection, and motionless I sat upon my bed with my head buried in my hands, for hours, days perhaps, for I could no longer measure time.

Then came the revulsion of feeling; the desire to be up and doing; the thirst for companionship. I would cry aloud, shriek, aye, even curse to drive away the madness that seemed to haunt the place, but all in vain; my own voice was not the one I longed to hear, and back would come that indefinable dread, that terrible something that told me I must save myself from despair or reason would desert me.

Whoever brought my food must have been under the strictest orders, for only a hand or arm was visible to me when the food was left. I have grabbed for that arm again and again, but what was my strength with his who came to me! How I have shrieked to him as his footsteps died away down the passage:

"Speak to me. In God's name speak to me, if you have a heart!"

Once only a mocking laugh came back to my ears, or seemed to, and for hours I imitated it, now in one corner and now in another, trying to imagine that my cell was filled with guests.

At other times I have pleaded, with tears and plaintive wailings, for just a word. Twice—thrice I have let him come and find my food untouched upon the shelf. Life was sustained with a crumb here and there, where it could be taken unnoticed. I hoped they might think me dead and I should at least see the face and hear the voice of my race once more. Famishing I lay upon my planks and heard the rusty chains clanking without. I did not stir. Two men appeared, and stalking to my side with a lantern, one of them exclaimed:

" Finished at last, I guess."

The other came to my side, placed his hand against my face, raised my arm, let it fall and turned to go out, saying:

" Making believe dead. He'll eat before to-morrow."

With this he threw the dried bread loaf, striking my face. With a cry of pain, I sprang upon him. The lantern was dashed to pieces. I would have struggled with him for no other reason but to change the routine of my life. I did not hate him. I thanked him for the pain he had given me. It seemed to begin a new life, a life of action, but he wrested himself from me, the heavy door swung together, I heard the chains fall clanking through the staples and again I was alone, *alone.*

Oh! you who wander forth into the blessed woodlands and say you have been alone; you who drift out from shore in an open boat, with your

eyes fixed upon the skies above you and say you
are alone, what can you know of such solitude as
mine, where not even the gnawing of a rat breaks
the unending silence. Hour after hour I toyed
with the broken pieces of the lantern. Each one
had its name; each to me was a living thing with
a personality of its own.

The little pin that held its door in place I would
throw away and then search for it. Again and
again I would throw it, hoping it would lodge in
some crevice and bring a new sensation when I
failed to find it in the accustomed places.

Wearied with this, I would count the hairs of
my beard, separating one from another and then
begin over again, assuming that the count had
been incorrect.

One day my food was thrust through the opening to me and in the meat a bone of peculiar
shape, not unlike a laborer's pick, gave rise to
thoughts which, for some strange reason, had never
visited me before. I kept it, and sharpening it
against the stones, began to dig away the wood on
the edge of my bed. I struck something hard.

Joy! The pinions were of iron. Here was a
hope, here was an occupation, here were the tools
to labor with. Oh! how I worked, and ere long
held in my hands six spikes, four inches long.
Day after day with these I picked and scraped and
dug at the stone wall of my cell until at last I
loosened a stone, then another and then another,
and then came to the moist earth. Again and
again I kissed that soil, calling it by endearing

names, as a mother would call a child that had been lost and restored. Using the fragments of stone to save my hands, I loosened the soil, filled the broken lantern and brought it back into my cell, filling the corners, stowing it away under the bed and spreading it on the planks where I slept. But my cell would not hold all the dirt I must move before I could hope to make an exit. I must have a place for it or all my labors would be in vain. Hoping against hope, I began to dig at the wall opposite the door. The spikes were almost worn away before the opening was made, but my efforts were not unavailing, for beyond the wall there had been, at some distant time, four cells like my own. These had been thrown into one. The doors had been walled up with solid masonry and it remained, I suppose, only as a support to the structure above.

Into this walled enclosure I packed away the earth as fast as I could loosen it and bring it back.

I had proceeded but twenty or thirty feet when I found a treasure of inestimable value to me, a broken sword, rusty and crumbling at the end and edges, but still substantial enough to serve in place of the worn-out spikes.

The hilt had once been richly jeweled, but most of the gems were gone. The few remaining I removed with a piece of broken stone and, wrapping them in a fragment of my clothing, treasured carefully in the fond hope that some day I should see the streets of London again. With this new implement, my work proceeded more favorably, and

using my own length as a measure, I estimated
that I had pushed along two hundred feet.

I then began to incline my course upward, and
ere many days had passed I knew by the quantity
of earth in the cells that I must be nearing the
surface. Onward and upward I crept, and yet no
sounds to tell me that I was nearing my goal. I
had stowed away all that I could. I would now
dig straight up and press the waste against the
sides of my tunnel by placing my back against
one side and crowding my feet hard against the
other, dropping handfuls of earth under them from
time to time.

Then came the thought. " May I not be under
the Thames! Will the swift influx of water flood
my cell and bear to them the unwritten story of
my struggles and my failure!"

I knew that I must be beyond the moat and beyond the double wall, if I had come out on the
side with the gates. It was my only hope, and
that failing me, death would be welcome, so I
pushed upward.

How my heart throbs as I recall that instant,
when, pushing through the turf, I felt the air of
heaven again blowing across my face! I had come
out into the open space diagonally across from the
tower gate. The stars were shining in the sky,
and now and then a cloud swept over the moon
as though to shroud my escape and cover my
flight.

Grasping what was left of the broken sword, I
climbed up to the level ground. Not a soul was

in sight. Lame and weak as I was, some strange, new-found power impelled me onward and I fled, not knowing, naught caring whither I was tending. If I met any one I do not know it. My blood seemed on fire. I was free. Let them take me back to-morrow if they would. I had tasted the air of freedom again and now I could die. On, on I went until, at last, nature, weak, worn and exhausted, left me panting at the door of an inn. I recall the keeper's burly form and red, good-natured face and then my senses must have left me for when I awoke I found myself in this bed. I have seen only the little girl who brought me materi. ls for writing and I have sent down the jewels from the sword hilt to compensate the inn-keeper for his care. I shall see him to-morrow and then I shall know if those who love me still live; if those for whom I have cared will now care for this broken reed that the storms of life have blasted. In the seventh house beyond the wooden bridge at Herne Hill road I left my wife and children. Shall I see them again! Shall I ever "——

Here the MS. breaks off, incomplete, and in a scrawling hand, probably that of the inn-keeper, are these words:

" Written by an old and ragged man, with long white hair and beard, who died in the kitchen chamber of the Blue Bird Inn. We have, as duty calls, sent to the seventh house from the wooden bridge, on Herne Hill road, but a happy family lives therein who seek no aged, dying man and know not who he may be. I place this packet in my strong box, where it shall lie until called for by him whom most it may concern. Signed, Berthold Willston."